Amy Redek

THE GOOD
TWELVE

12 STORIES
IN ONE

WARNING

This book contains sexually explicit scenes and adult language. It may be considered offensive to some readers. This book is for sale to adults ONLY.

Please store your files wisely where they cannot be accessed by underage readers.

* * * * * * * * * * * * * * * * * * * *

WANT FREE COPIES OF MY BOOKS?
Just visit my blog and download free copies of my books:
amy-redek.awesomeauthors.org/amy-redek

About the Publisher

4Fun Publishing, a member of **BLVNP Incorporated**, 340 S. Lemon #6200, Walnut CA 91789, info@blvnp.com / legal@blvnp.com
NOTE: Due to the highly emotional reaction of some people to works of erotic fiction, any email sent to the above address that contains foul language or religious references is automatically deleted by our anti-spam software and will not be seen. All other communications are welcome.

DISCLAIMER

Please don't be stupid and kill yourself. This book is a work of FICTION. Do not try any new sexual practice that you find in this book. It is fiction and not to be confused with reality. Neither the author nor the publisher or its associates assume any responsibility for any loss, injury, death or legal consequences resulting from acting on the contents in this book. Every character in this book is over 18 years of age. The author's opinions are not to be construed as the opinions of the publisher. The material in this book is for entertainment purposes ONLY. Enjoy.

The Good Twelve

12 Stories in One

By: Amy Redek

ISBN: 978-1-68030-335-3

12 Stories in 1

Gone Fishing

High Court

The Last Carriage

The Lemon Trees

Tom

Traffic Cop

Where's Daddy?

Minty

I Wish

Never Again

Spelling and Words

Gremlin

Gone Fishing

My father passed away about a year ago and so I was now alone in my house for my mother had walked out from us many years ago when I was only a child of five. The reason for that my father told me later, was because of him being caught getting another woman pregnant. After an awful row, she had left us, leaving father to raise me on his own.

It was disappointing not to have my mother around but he looked after me well enough in seeing that I was brought up properly. He often took me fishing on the river that ran past the bottom of our garden where we had a boathouse that held our small boat. I say boathouse though it was not a proper one but more of a large shed that covered a small inlet into our garden.

The river was called the Pax and our house was on the outskirts of the town of Paxham, having taken its name from the river when it was just a small hamlet. The boat, which I never did know what type it should be called, was quite deep in the middle and had a small outboard motor attached. I liked this boat because of the inside depth of it for when I took my girlfriend out in it for fishing, it was easy for us to lie down in the bottom of it for us to kiss and cuddle and not be seen when anchored out in the middle of the river.

There was one particular spot about a mile and a half down river where for a stretch of at least fifty yards on either bank, gorse bushes came right down to the river's edge and so it was unlikely that persons on the banks could get down to the river and see my boat anchored and us kissing there.

On this particular day, I was now twenty six years of age and my girlfriend, Josie, was twenty one. I loved our kissing of each other and found the courage to ask if she would marry me. I was over the moon when she said yes. I then saw that it was time to return to our houses and so began to pull up the small light anchor that had held the boat still in the slowly moving river.

'It's caught on something,' I said, having difficulty in upping the anchor and she moved to the bow to give me a hand. With both of us pulling on the anchor's rope, it slowly began to come up but we didn't get it out of the river. For as we slowly gathered the rope in we found what it had caught and Josie gave out a scream and we both let go of the rope to sink back down with what the anchor had attached itself to, for we had seen the head of a skeleton!

'Christ Almighty,' I had exclaimed, turning round to hold a shaking Josie and calm her down at her having seen what had once been a living person. What I then did was to get the empty bottle of water he still had in the boat and tied this to the anchor rope that I had cut free and let it float on top of the water to show where this skeleton was.

It was a silent pair that was in the boat as I got the engine running and moved it back upstream to my house where, after mooring the boat, phoned the police to tell them of what we had found. About an hour later, I was being interviewed by two police officers, one of them being a woman, and knew both of them as they were locals like me. They said that after they had got hold of a diver and a boat, they would collect me to show them where in the river I had anchored, which they did.

So with them collecting me, and with their boat being more powerful than mine, we're soon down where I had anchored and found the floating bottle. Now the diver went over the side and two minutes later was back up and confirmed that there was indeed a skeleton anchored below by what looked like a roadside grating. This was confirmed after they had recovered the remains of which I had no part for they had left me behind when they did this later in the day, but was told of this the following day when I gave a full statement down at the local nick.

Two divers had gone down, one to lift the skeleton and one the grating that was chained to the legs. Between them, they got both to the surface where others took over to get them into the boat where they were taken to the town for an autopsy. I queried this word asking how can you do an autopsy on a skeleton? I thought that it had to have flesh for this to be carried out but was told that bones could still be identified by any bone marrow left, the pelvic bones and teeth. They guessed that it could be somebody local for the grating was of the same style as that used in the town to drain off the rain water from the roads.

Well the pelvic bones told them that it was of a female and they could also start checking with the teeth because of the possibility of it being a local woman and these teeth being noted at some dentist's records. It took a few weeks but they found a match which shocked me, for the woman's name was Joan Redmond. I haven't told you yet that my name is Jack Redmond and this was most likely the bones of my mother that I had hooked onto.

I was in shock!

Could this really have been my mother who was supposed to have walked out from our home twenty one years ago? There was only one way to find out and agreed for them to do a D.N.A. test on me to see if it was a match to the bones of the woman. This didn't take long to confirm that there was a match and it was indeed that of my mother.

Now this raised another question, apart from the fact that my father must have murdered her, though how, they couldn't say, and chained her legs to the grating and dumped her there and put out the story that she had left him because of him getting another woman pregnant. When the news broke out in the town, the question came from the mother of Josie who claimed that it was my father, John Redmond who had gotten her pregnant and therefore requested that Josie went through D.N.A. testing to compare it with mine. This they did and it was confirmed that she was indeed the daughter of my father.

So there was I, engaged to Josie, but now we couldn't get married because she was in fact my half sister!

End of the 1st Story

High Court

'I am arresting you for the murder of Robert Smith. Whatever you say will be taken down and may be used in evidence etc....'

I was astounded. One minute I'm planning the deed, and the next, I'm getting arrested for doing it. It was strange that the arresting officer was in a uniform that I'd never seen before. All in white with gold buttons down the front and on the pockets, and shiny gold bars on top of his shoulders.

I wasn't handcuffed, but still escorted by two other similarly dressed policemen, and conducted to a whitewashed cell. There was only a thin mattress covered bed and a chair in there and one small barred window. I went up onto my toes to look out, hoping to see blue sky, but all I could see were fleecy white clouds that sedately rolled past. I sat down to contemplate my fate. I noticed that some wag had done a crude drawing of a devil, pointed ears and a spiky tail. He held a trident in his hand which was pointing down to what I took to be drawings of flames in what I assumed to be hell. This was the only graffiti in the cell, so it wasn't a place that Kilroy had visited.

They certainly move fast here I thought as I was soon ushered up some steps into a courtroom. It was pretty much the same as any court in England, except instead of wearing black gowns, those there were wearing white ones. Even the judge I noticed was dressed the same. I was expecting him to be wearing the scarlet ermine robes that I'd always seen depicted in films. He even had a beard that was so white, I couldn't see how long or wide it was because it seemed to meld into his gown. He looked at me, or I should say peered, through his thin glass spectacles that looked in danger of falling off the end of his nose.

'You have been brought here before this court for a most heinous of crimes. We do not ask you to plead as to whether you are guilty or not, because that you are here is sufficient in your particular case. All I do here is sentence you, and with the agreement of your counsel and the prosecutor, will do so. You will be sent to the rehabilitation centre for lost souls, to serve your time there until your case is reviewed in the next millennium. It is only your past behaviour that has brought you here, because to us, the taking of any mortal soul is a crime, and suicide, we regard as murder, Mister Robert Smith.'

The End

The Last Carriage

I checked my watch and I was on time as usual as I showed my travel pass to the ticket inspector, and I made my way to the platform for my train from Grant Road Station to the next town down the line, Waverley. This was where I lived and it was only a thirty minute journey. I had bought the evening paper as I always did at the kiosk, wondering for the umpteenth time as to why it was called an evening paper when it was obviously printed in the late morning for it to be sold at this time in the early evening. I suppose it was because you could only buy it at this time of day though it was usually a rehash of what was in the morning papers.

I walked onto the platform and the train was still standing there with its doors open. They must be getting cold inside I thought, for the wind was getting up and it being just a few days into the New Year. The snow had settled during the day and was now crusty underfoot and very slippery as the ice formed as were all the roads making driving very hazardous.

I sat in my usual seat in the last carriage and looked at my watch again to see that I was on time, it being six twenty five precisely. A few other people got on and sat down as I began to read my paper. The train doors made a quiet hissing noise as they slid shut and the train moved slowly off without any sense of it being in motion a couple of moments later. The only noticeable thing was the fact that the wind had stopped blowing into the carriage.

I read the sports section on the back page first because tonight was the home football match against an old rival team. As usual, this pundit spent half the article telling you why the home team should win, and the other half was how they could lose. This then meant that in the paper next day, he could quote from whichever half of this article he wanted to use to say that he had told us what the outcome would be.

I turned the paper over and had a queer sensation touch me that all was not as it seemed to be, and I couldn't really shake off this sense of unease. I looked up from the headlines, which was only really saying that of the morning's paper, to try and see if I could make out what was causing me to have these feelings of misgiving. Something was missing and I couldn't quite put my finger on it.

I looked out of the window at the snow covered fields, hearing the clickety clack, clickety clack as the trains sped along the track. Then it struck me of what I was not hearing! Nobody was talking to a friend, neighbour or fellow passenger. No mobile phones were sending out their silly little tunes to give out silly little messages. It was the first week of January and nobody had a cold, or at least sniffing or giving out a hacking cough. There wasn't any of the passengers that I could see, reading a newspaper, rustling it as they turned over a page, or looking at a book. They all were just sitting there, staring at each other, lost in little worlds of their own.

I then noticed their pallor, the white skin of their faces and the dull listlessness of their eyes. No sunshine and being bored to death with their jobs was my first thought. Even the man sitting opposite me appeared to look at me with dead dark staring eyes, not seeing me at all, but seemed to not be there at all. Even this last carriage of the train seemed colder than usual until I realised that the heating system couldn't be working.

I tried to shake of this feeling of foreboding as I again started to read my newspaper, and then the stop press section caught my eye.

'Local train disaster! The six twenty eight train from Grant Road was in collision with a juggernaut truck. In all, twenty passengers were killed.'

It didn't register at first. I looked up and idly counted the number of people I could see and got to the figure of nineteen. It said twenty I said to myself and then shot bolt upright. With me it made twenty! I hastily scanned the date of the paper and saw that it was indeed today's newspaper, and we had left Grant Road at precisely six twenty eight. I crushed the paper in my hands in confusion as my mind tried to grasp what I had just read. How could it report in the latter hours of the morning of a crash that allegedly happens later that evening?

I panicked and lifted my arm and pulled the emergency chain and a few seconds later came the screeching sounds of the brakes being applied to the metal wheels of the train. I sat there as the train slowed and looked at my paper to see the stop press item start to fade away till there was just a blank space left. All the passengers were looking at me, even those who had their backs to me, turned round, their blank, dark dead eyes staring at me. I looked up at the chain I still held in my hand and read the warning notice that was printed below it.

'For wanton or improper use of the emergency alarm system, the penalty is death.'

I couldn't tear my eyes away from this sign as the train came to a halt. It was then that I saw that we had come to a stop, our carriage, the last one of the train, was astride the road crossing of Memorial Drive. The barrier was down, but that was not going to stop the forty foot truck and trailer that had just jack-knifed on the road and was sliding on the icy road towards us.

As it crashed through the road barrier, I gave one last despairing look at the blank dead faces looking accusingly at me as I hung onto that emergency cord and tried to brace myself for its inevitable collision with the last carriage.

* * *

Author's note: This story of a dream was told to me three weeks before a passenger train was hit by a juggernaut, killing twenty people in the last carriage.
Déjà vu?

The End

The Lemon Trees

During the Spanish Civil War, Jose Garcia was a leader of a small band of Loyalists. Fortunately for him, he operated outside of his own region so that when this war was over, he was able to return to his small farm without anyone the wiser as to which side he had been on.

He had operated in the hills and was a constant thorn in the side of the German troops that were fighting for the Insurgents. What with their ambushes and hit and run tactics, they didn't take prisoners. Jose personally executed them, even a young pilot that had been shot down. They were never caught and lived to see out the end of this civil war, before, disgruntled, disbanded to make their way to their respective homes.

So Jose got back to his farm, though in fact it was really just fields that he didn't fancy ploughing and growing crops. So he turned these fields into one massive orchard and planted orange trees. Being basically a lazy man, he was quite content with the small living he made from the fruit that was harvested and sent off to the markets nearby. What little profit he did make, was put back into planting a few more trees every year.

He never married and was happy enough to just spend his time wandering through the orchard, seeing the lovely orange blossoms turn into fruit that would be turned into money to live on and the rest put back into the orchard.

The seasons passed and it was nearly twenty years after the war that while walking through the trees that he found a young man inspecting some of the trees.

'What are you doing here?' Jose demanded. 'This is private property.'

'Please forgive me,' the young man said. 'I was passing by and couldn't help but stop to admire the orchard here. Ever since I was a little boy, I've studied fruit trees. I even went to our Horticultural College and got a degree in this field. My name is John Smith, from England. I'm on a year's vacation and I'm spending it here in Spain, looking at orchards such as this one of yours.'

'You speak Spanish very well for an Englishman,' Jose said as he introduced himself. 'You are quite welcome then to look as you like at my trees. I've been growing them myself for the past twenty years,' he said quite proudly.

'Yes, I can see that, because some of your trees have pomarium fructus robigo.'

'Pardon?' Jose said, rather perplexed at this.

'Blight. Some of the trees are infected with this fruit blight. I've noticed quite a few already suffering from this and need to be cleared or you will eventually lose the orchard.'

'I've not noticed anything wrong with them,' Jose said.

'That's my specialty. I would take the infected trees out and replace them with lemon trees.'

'Lemon trees? What good would that do?' Jose asked, being ignorant of this so called blight.

'Well the acidity in the tree itself, will prevent this blight from spreading and thereby save the orchard. Surely you can still sell lemons in the market as well as oranges?'

'Yes, but I don't really know how to go about doing this.'

'Well I've got nearly a whole year before I return to my university, if you could give me lodgings and food here, I could help,' John offered.

'That's very kind of you, I accept,' Jose said with a big smile on his face.

* * *

So John stayed at the farm with Jose for six months, picking out great swathes of trees and getting them out of the ground for burning. Jose, borrowing money from the bank against future crop sales, bought young lemon trees and helped John plant them in the same place where once orange trees grew.

They laboured every day of that six months until John said that it was all done and that they could now sit back and relax.

'I hope that all this has been worthwhile. I've gone into debt and it will take me quite a few years to pay back the loans,' Jose told him.

'Oh it will be worthwhile, I can assure you. I've really enjoyed doing this most rewarding work and you will be astonished at the outcome,' John said to him, and the next day, he packed his haversack and said farewell to Jose who returned back to his isolated style of living. He still kept wandering around the orchard, liking the display of yellow amongst the orange and found it pleasing to the eye. It was a bountiful crop that year and he was most happy.

*　*　*

It was two years later that three men came to the farmhouse of Jose and introduced themselves. One being the mayor of the town who Jose knew and the other two being from the government.

'We've been sent some material,' one of the latter said, opening his briefcase and pulled out a folder, 'that we'd like you to explain.'

Jose looked bewildered as he was handed an old photograph.

'Do you know this man?' the man asked of him. It was a faded snapshot of a smiling young man in flying overalls standing next to a small bi-plane.

'No,' Jose replied, handing it back.

'Or this one?' being handed a second photograph. This too was of a young man smiling for the camera.

'Why yes. This is a picture of John Smith. An Englishman who helped me awhile back.'

'Well his real name is Johann Schmidt from Germany and the previous picture was of his father, Hans Schmidt. A pilot who was executed during the civil war.'

Jose began to tremble, wondering what was coming next as another photograph was being presented to him.

'We have been sent sworn statements from witnesses that you personally shot this man in the first photograph, but it is this picture,' which he handed to Jose, 'that you are now holding that is causing us the utmost concern at the gravity of it.'

Jose, his hand now trembling even more, looked at the picture and saw that it was an aerial photograph of his orchard, and gasped. In the middle of the orange and green could be clearly seen, picked out in a different shade of green and bright yellow, a symbol. It was the zig zag form of a swastika, the hated symbol of Nazism.

'That was you see, is of your orchard. This symbol is forbidden and therefore it is to be destroyed. Here is a copy of the order from the government to that effect.'

With that, the three men left and two bulldozers moved in and completely destroyed the whole orchard as Jose watched in tears. Heavily in debt he was now a ruined man, and when Johann Schmidt, alias John Smith read of this a few days later, smiled and said out loud to himself. 'The lemon is bitter, but vengeance is sweet.'

The End

Tom

I was orphaned at an early age and was most fortunate to be taken in by Peter and Mary Withers, for I took the place of the child they never had.

Peter was the gamekeeper for Lord Carlton on his estate in Wiltshire and Mary helped out in the house when they had guests, which was mostly in the shooting season. We lived in the lodge at the entrance to the estate and were about a mile from the small village down the lane.

I was happy there as I grew up and Peter saw to my schooling for there was nowhere else I could go for this. Being the gamekeeper, he knew all about animals and birds that lived out in the woods and fields and when I went out with him, he would point out the different species and how to track them. Though part of his job was to keep the poachers at bay and stop them from snaring the pheasants and grouse.

It was some years before he would take me out with him on his nightly prowls, moving quietly to try and find traps that the poachers would set up in the woods. I got to learn the most likely places they would be set and I was quite pleased when I did find one.

'Well done Tom,' he would cry and ruffle the hair of my head, a habit of his for I was far shorter than he was.

One of the turning points of my life was when I was allowed to go into the pub with him. I'd been refused entry before because I was too small but now that I was growing up, they turned a blind eye to me going in with him as long as I behaved myself.

I used to like those evenings, though it was only twice a week. We'd have our dinner and then we'd set off for the pub in the village which was a good mile down the lane. It was only a small place, but now that I was older, they let me in and it was Old Percy who bought me my first beer. It was only half a pint of bitter, but it made the night for me to drink with the locals.

Peter and I would settle ourselves by the log fire and though I didn't smoke or wouldn't have been allowed to anyway, I did like the smell of his pipe when he lit it. He would stretch out his legs and puff away and I would stretch my feet out too and listen to the older men talk.

Though most of what they talked about went over my head and after drinking my small half pint of beer, I would drowse in front of the fire only catching half of what they said. Peter would have maybe three pints but drew the line with me, saying that half was enough. In spite of this restriction on my drinking, I still enjoyed those evenings.

Come ten o'clock, he would finish his beer and wake me up and tell me it was time for bed and that I couldn't sleep in the pub. We would then walk the mile back home and invariable, Mary would be in bed but she always left us a little something to eat before we went to bed. I think she would have been annoyed if she knew that Peter was letting me drink beer when I was out with him.

*   *   *

Those were happy years and I really began to get the knack of catching rabbits which Mary was pleased with and so we would quite often have rabbit stew and it was a meal I never got tired of. I learned a lot out in the woods with Peter, all about the predators such as foxes and the like that would try and flush out the grouse to catch and eat them, but I was never taught about others than the poachers. This I learned when our own coop was invaded.

Peter and I had just been down in the pub and Old Percy, bless him, sneaked me another beer this particular evening and I even got a case of the hiccups from drinking it too fast. We left at the usual time of ten o'clock and with the mile walk home, it sobered me up. We had our evening snack and then I went to my bed while he went to his.

I'm sure it was the walk home and the sobering up after having a whole pint of beer which a twelve year old shouldn't be having, that I came awake at a strange sound in the house. Now I won't say that I'm brave, but the noise I heard wasn't normal, so I got up from my bed and began to investigate the cause of the disturbance. With hindsight, I should have woken up Peter and Mary, but I went and looked for myself.

It was in the small dining room that I saw this figure of a man, waving his torch about as he looked at the china cabinet before going to the drawer where the silver cutlery was kept.

Stealing the silver!

That was enough for me, I might have only been twelve years old but I went charging at him.

I head butted him in the stomach and such was the surprise of our bodies coming together, that he fell over with me on top of him. Boy, did we make a noise as we crashed into the chairs by the table. He swung at me with his torch but I managed to catch hold of his arm as I lay on his chest. It didn't stop him from giving me two hefty punches into my ribs with his free hand.

The lights had come on with the noise we had made and I heard Peter come down the stairs as I still fought to hold onto the burglar's arm.

'Okay Tom,' Peter said. 'I've got him,' and gave this burglar a hefty right fist straight to the jaw. As the man went limp under me, I let go of his arm, panting for breath as he'd knocked all the wind out of me. 'You're crazy! Do you know that Tom? He could have killed you. Now go and sit down and let me deal with him.'

For that, I was grateful. I got myself over to the sofa and sat down, still trying to get my wind back, my ribs really hurting me now from the burglar's blows.

Peter went to the phone and dialed a number which I guessed was to Sydney, our village policeman. He lived at the station, well it wasn't exactly a police station for it was his house that doubled up as one.

'Yes, he's out cold but collect him as quick as you can,' he said before putting the phone down.

It was a good five to ten minutes before we heard Sydney's car pull up outside and a minute later, Sydney was in the parlour.

'Who is it?' he asked.

'That bloody Alfred. Caught him enough times poaching, now he's doing this stealing from us,' Peter said.

'Well he'll probably be sent down for this, it's not the first time. You did a good job of catching him in the act,' Sydney said.

'It wasn't me,' Peter replied. 'It was Tom.' I got up and went over to where Sydney was just putting a pair of handcuffs on Alfred. He straightened up and did as Peter often did, ruffling the hair of my head.

'Well done Tom!' Which made me smile. I watched as Alfred was dragged up onto his feet as he was coming round now from the good punch that Peter had given him, and we watched as he was bundled into Sydney's car to be taken away.

We went back inside and I went and sat back down on the sofa and Peter came and sat next to me.

'Yes, you did a good job there Tom,' he said as he ruffled my hair again. 'Mary and I both love you, for you really are a good dog.'

The End

Traffic Cop

'Come on, hurry or we'll miss the plane.'

I'd just paid the hotel bill and was seeing to the luggage being piled into the trunk of the hired car. I urged the wife into the front seat and the two disgruntled children into the back. They didn't want to go home after two lovely weeks of sunshine, beach and pool.

'We'd cut it fine for me to get the car to the airport, hand it over and get checked in for our flight back to England, so I was a bit heavy on the throttle as we left the hotel.

I'd cleared the town and was out on the main road and then got stuck behind another car on a series of bends. Then came an open stretch and it wasn't far to the next no overtaking sign, so I floored the pedal. Would you believe it! The car in front started to accelerate just as I was overtaking him, so I was a good thirty yards past this sign before I got in front of him.

Then all of a sudden, there are two police motorcycles alongside of me and the one closest to me was waving and pointing to the side of the road. Well I won't say the words I used at that point as I slowed down and drifted off to the side of the road with them just stopping just ahead of me. I got a merry toot from the car that I'd overtaken as he went sailing along at a sedate speed.

The policeman who had waved me down had put his bike up on to its stand and began to walk slowly back towards me, his notebook out and obviously noting down the car's number plate. I wound down my window as he approached.

'Leave me to do the talking,' I said to the wife. 'I'll sort this out.'

The officer stopped and spoke to me in rapid Spanish, not understanding a single word he'd said. I rallied up the one sentence that I knew in Spanish.

'No habla Español Senor.' My only other words being, yes, thank you, what, and beer.

'¿Inglése?'

'Yes, si.'

'Do you know sir, that you overtook that car crossing a solid white line while you did so?' he said in perfect English.

'I would have been alright if the fool hadn't accelerated just as I was about to pass him,' I said.

'Be that as it may sir, you should have slowed down and fell in behind him till you had a safer place to overtake,' the cop said.

'Yes sir, I realise that now. May I say that you speak very good English.'

'Thank you. I spent two years in England, but I prefer the sunshine as you obviously do too.'

'Where abouts did you stay in England?' I asked, giving him a pleasant smile.

'In London.'

'Did you really? I work in London, and, I might add, helping traffic police like you. Guiding traffic when they're busy. I'm a traffic warden.' I shot a smug smile at the wife to show how I was getting along so well with him.

'Are you really? Do you know that for my two years there at the Police Academy, I was constantly being harassed by traffic wardens. You can't park here, you can't park there. They used to laugh at my accent as I was learning the language. The wheel is half over the line he would say as he wrote me a ticket. I demonstrated of course, but he replied that he was adhering to the law. A lovely phrase that, adhering to the law. So I am adhering to the law now. You have just violated one of our rules of the road by overtaking another vehicle where it is forbidden. Also, when you passed through the town just now, you ran a red light.'

'It was a pedestrian crossing and there wasn't anybody in sight!' I protested.

'Be that as it may be sir. The red light means stop, which you didn't do. Also, you exceeded the forty kilometre speed limit twice when passing through. Now let's see what that adds up to in fines. Oh dear, I'm a little short to round it up to a nice tidy sum. Surely you must have done something else?'

'Oh this is damn stupid! Don't be so bloody ridiculous!'

'Ah, thank you sir. Insulting a police officer in the course of his duties,' he said, noting this down in his book. 'That rounds it off nicely.'

He placed both hands on the door and leaned slightly towards me. 'That brings the fine up to one thousand Euros, cash! If you do not pay, we will impound the vehicle until it is and you will most certainly miss your flight.'

'You can't do this! We don't do this in England!'

'True sir, but you are now here in Spain.'

The End

Where's Daddy?

'Where's daddy?' Jenny queried of her mother when they entered the kitchen. She had just been collected from school, the last day of term before Christmas. She was clutching her books and the special pictures that she had drawn for her father.

'He's at work darling,' her mother replied.

'But I want him to see my pictures,' she said with a catch in her voice.

'He'll see them when he comes home,' mother said, bustling about the kitchen, getting tea ready for Jenny.

'He's never at home when I want him,' she muttered under her breath as she left the kitchen to go into the lounge. At six years of age, she wanted the approbation of her father on the pictures she had spent, to her, laborious hours drawing before colouring them in. She went to his favourite chair by the fire and curled up in it, hugging the cushion to her small chest, inhaling the special aroma of himself and his pipe tobacco.

Mother called her back into the kitchen half an hour later, and sat down with her as she ate her tea, which really was supper, because when she'd finished, it was time for her bath. After which and while being put into bed, she again asked of her mother.

'Where's daddy?'

'I told you darling. He's working, but he'll look in when he comes home.' So after her goodnight kiss, Jenny snuggled down in the bed, wishing that her father would come home.

* * *

Next morning after breakfast. Jenny and her mother wrapped themselves up and went down to the Mall so that she could spend her pocket money on buying her father his Christmas present. She picked out a new pipe that she thought he would like, and when she presented it at the counter along with her money, she asked the assistant, 'Have you seen my daddy?'

The answer she got was no, and so with the pipe wrapped up in colourful Christmas paper, they left the shop. But even then on the way home, Jenny had to stop to ask the man selling newspapers on the corner if he had seen her daddy. With a negative answer, she was disconsolate as her mother started to hurry her as the snow was beginning to fall, rather thick and fast. It was with some relief that they got home and were back in the warmth.

It was a light lunch they had and Jenny spent the rest of the day sitting in her father's chair before the fire with her pictures. Mother picked her up and carried her through to the kitchen for her supper and sat with her as she always did till she was finished. Then it was bath time again. With the bathing done, she was rubbed down and dried with a nice warm towel and then helped into her nightgown.

'Pop along and into bed darling, and I'll come along as soon as I've cleaned up this pretty mess we've made here.'

Jenny left the bathroom, but instead of going to her room, she went downstairs and opened the front door and went out into the snow. She went down the path and out onto the snow covered pavement.

'Where on earth do you think you are going dressed like that?' asked a young woman who, bending down, stopped her from going any further.

'I'm looking for my daddy,' she replied.

'Jenny? Jenny? Came the frantic call from the house as her mother came flying out of the open front door. The young woman took hold of Jenny's hand and straightened up so that she could be seen beyond the hedge.

'I think this is who you are looking for,' she called out. Jenny's mother rushed out and gathered Jenny into her arms.

'You silly, silly girl,' she cried, tears in her eyes. Turning to the young woman, she said her thanks for stopping Jenny from going any further out in the snow. Then she whisked the cold child back indoors, into the warm and after rubbing her cold feet, put her to bed with kisses and tears.

'What on earth did you think you were doing you silly little goose?'

'I wanted to see if I could find daddy,' Jenny said with tears in her voice as well as in her eyes.

'You'll see him soon darling, but don't wander out like that in the cold snow again. Now go to sleep and I promise you that daddy will look in to see you when he gets home from work.'

*   *   *

The snow fell heavily all the next day, and Jenny, very listlessly, watched it fall and pile up on the garden path. It was the following day that was of great concern for her mother. Jenny was running a high temperature and she had a wheezy cough and complained of pains in her chest. Wrapped up very warmly, her mother took her down to the doctor's surgery for advice. After the usual wait, not having made an appointment, they eventually got in to see the doctor.

'Well we do have a hot little girl here,' he said, getting a thermometer out from its small case. 'Let's put this under your tongue, but you mustn't bite it. It tastes terrible. Now let's hear what's going on inside you.' Mother pulled up her jumper and vest for the doctor to place his stethoscope against her chest.

'S' cold,' Jenny burbled around the thermometer.

'That's because you are so hot,' the doctor replied. 'Now let's hear from the back,' he said as he moved round. Then taking the earpieces out and letting them hang round his neck, took the small tube from her mouth and looked at it before putting it down and started to write on a pad that was on his desk.

'She has a very high temperature and a chest infection. It's not that serious at the moment, but I would like you to take her to the hospital for them to check her out properly. They can then give her antibiotics for her chest and some medicine to bring down her temperature.'

So after thanking the doctor, off to the hospital went mother and Jenny where she was told that it wasn't that serious, but it was better to be safe than sorry by saying that they would keep her in for the night for observation. Jenny couldn't resist asking the doctor there as she had done of the doctor in the surgery, if he had seen her daddy. A nurse took them to the children's ward where they saw a huge Christmas tree at the far end and all decorated with lots of fairly lights and coloured baubles, and hanging from the ceiling, lots of little stars covered in silver paper.

Jenny was undressed by her mother and put into one of the beds when suddenly, the lights went down, leaving the Christmas tree to give out the only illumination to the ward. The little silver stars now shone and sparkled as they reflected the tree lights, just like stars in the sky. There was then a flurry of activity in the doorway to the ward, and a big burly figure came through the swing doors.

'Ho, Ho, Ho,' he cried, and all the children saw that it was Santa Claus that had come into the ward. With a big full sack, he went down one side of the ward giving out presents to the children in those beds. He reached the end where the tree was and sat down and wiped his forehead with a great big red handkerchief.

'Merry Christmas,' he cried, and then he beckoned towards Jenny. She looked up at her mother who nodded and helped her from the bed. Jenny took it slowly, walking across the floor to Santa, who held out his arms and lifted her upon to his lap.

She looked up into the twinkling eyes above his big white whiskers and then cuddled in close to him. She recognised the eyes and the smell of his pipe tobacco and knew that she had found her daddy.

The End

Minty

I lost my husband nearly eighteen years ago. It was most unfortunate him being on the motorway where he was caught in the middle of a horrendous pile up. I would often sit out in the garden of an evening, wishing that he was still with me, for I was so lonely. I didn't want another man because I would constantly be comparing the two, so still wanted some sort of comfort I decided to get a lovely little kitten.

She would romp around the garden and then come and jump onto my lap for me to stroke her and she would purr when giving my hand a lick. The reason I picked her out of the litter was that on one side of her body she was nearly black but had a white ring which reminded me of the peppermint that I used to buy when I was much younger and so I named her Minty.

She always tried to please me in everything she did, especially when I went outside to sit down on the bench that I used to share with my husband. To give you the picture, in the middle of the lawn, he built a little lighthouse. No, that's wrong really, for it wasn't a lighthouse, it was a square of bricks, four high and on top of this he placed a lamp. Just like those they used back in the early nineties to light up the streets, but this was only a few feet above the ground.

I would switch it on in the evening before going out to sit on our bench and look back to the past. It was this that seemed to fascinate Minty, for she would race round the lamp and as a finale, would jump up and perch herself on the top. With me clapping my hands, she would jump down and come and jump up onto my lap. Mind you, this was only in the summer and autumn. It was pleasant to see the sun go down and yet still be warm.

Minty could be a right minx sometimes, especially when I sat there knitting, she would knock the ball of wool off my lap and push it around the garden, it would unwind making me put down my knitting to chase after her and the unravelling wool.

It was fun really and I think we both loved the pleasure it gave us, and it lasted fourteen years. For that was her age when she died one morning. I was heartbroken at not seeing her in the kitchen waiting for her breakfast. Fearing the worst, it wasn't long before I found out the reality of my fears.

I cried when I saw her lying in front of the lighthouse, but not moving or answering my call and I went over and fell down onto my knees and picked her up and cuddled my little friend who had now passed on. It was with a heavy heart that I laid her to one side to go and get a spade from the shed. This I used to dig where I had found her lying.

I didn't have breakfast that morning for I couldn't have eaten a thing and I dug down into the earth until it was at least five feet deep. I cast the spade to one side and went into the house to find an old Christmas sweets tin, also collecting her little blanket that she slept on at night and took both things back out into the garden. With the lid of the tin off, I put her blanket inside, having the outer parts draping over the sides. I then, sorrowfully picked up Minty and laid her down inside, making her as comfortable as I could before covering her up with her blanket after kissing her goodbye. With her settled inside, I put the lid back on the tin and sealed it with some tape before putting it into the hole that I had dug, which was now to be her grave.

I cried the whole time I was pushing the earth back to cover the tin until the hole was filled. I pressed the earth down and covered the earth with parts of the lawn that I had removed before digging the hole. In the shed, my late husband had quite a few letters of the alphabet that was to have been used for him to make a name plate for our house. It never got done, but the letters that I wanted were there, so mixing up some sticky paste, I took the letters that I wanted and stuck them to the bricks of the lighthouse, them spelling out the name of Minty.

It was sometime later I went out into the garden, having turned on the lighthouse and sat down on the bench. Looking up, I saw something on top of the lamp and when it moved, I saw that it was a little kitten. It jumped down on seeing me and came running over and jumped up onto my lap. It was then that I saw on her side, one white ring and knew that Minty had come back to me.

The End

I Wish

Before I reached my eleventh birthday, I really believed I was a witch. It was on that day that I found out that I wasn't but that I had a strange gift of being able to make one wish a year that would turn out to come true.

My first recollection of this was after my fifth birthday, just after I had started school. I saw that another girl had brought a doll to class and it was one that I had seen in the toyshop in town. Now I had wanted this doll badly and nearly cried when I found that my birthday presents were nearly all new clothes as I would now be starting school. There were a couple of toys but not this doll.

'Can I play with your doll?' I asked this other girl.

'No Mandy,' she said, holding it very tight in case I should try to take it away from her.

She called me Mandy for that was my name, well not really, for it had been shortened from Amanda. Amanda Beatrice Clarkson. I lived in a semi-detached house that my father had bought, though sadly, I cannot remember him for he died when I was two. This had left us in dire straits for father's insurance wasn't that large and was only just enough to keep up with the mortgage payments, so mother had to go back out to work.

But back to that doll. With being refused to be even allowed to touch it, I said, 'I wish my mother had bought that doll for me.' It was the usual wistful wish that many children make but it was different for me.

Two days later after being picked up when school was over for the day and being driven to my babysitter for mother to go to work, she said she had another present for me. I looked over onto the back seat to see a wrapped up parcel and as I was dropped off, it was given to me. My heart leapt for joy and tears came to my eyes when I unwrapped it to find this precious doll that I had wished for. I gave her lots of kisses for it and promised to be good. My sixth year wish was a foolish one on reflection for I was having my birthday party with a few friends round and one particular girl was being rather obnoxious which prompted me to wish that she hadn't come and leave and never come back.

Within an hour, she was collected by her parents and a few days later, the whole family moved and I never saw her again. Any other amount of wishing during the next year didn't bring about any changes and it slowly began to dawn on me that maybe I was only being allowed one wish a year and that seemed to coincide with my birthday. I went back over my short years and tried to remember what I had wished for, when and what happened, and could only come up with that answer.

Having convinced myself of this, it was with some trepidation that I waited for my ninth birthday and resolved to keep my mouth shut in terms of wishes until I knew exactly what I would wish for and see if it happened. Mother scraped up enough money to give me a small party, she apologised that the presents she gave me were paltry compared to what she would have loved to have given me. I told her not to worry for you never know what's round the corner and so when I was alone in my bedroom that night, I made my wish.

'I wish we could come into some money so that mother doesn't have to worry anymore about not having enough.' It was almost like saying a prayer for I had knelt down by my bed as I said my wish before getting inside and going to sleep.

Two days later, I was in the local paper shop getting what they obviously sold and turning away from the counter saw a scratch card lying on the floor. I quickly picked it up seeing that it hadn't had the little silver parts scratched off. I looked round to see if anyone had seen me pick this ticket up and as no one seemed to take any notice of me, hurried out and went back home. Was this my wish coming true, I whispered to myself as I dropped the newspaper on the kitchen table and went up to my bedroom and laid the card on the bed.

Golden Chance it had blazed across the top. You can win up to half a million pounds, it read and thought that would be going too far, but I would settle for whatever if it was a winning ticket and bring us some money. So I got out my nail file and slowly began to scrape off this silver covering of six numbers. When I found that I had five of the six numbers that had been printed at the bottom I was over the moon. I couldn't wait to scratch off the section to say what the prize would be for having five out six and gasped when as I scratched away from right to left and uncovered noughts up to five and then reveal a one. Ten thousand pounds! That's when I believed I was a witch!

My mother gasped after taking it and gave me a big hug. Then came the questions. Did I buy it or steal it?

'No mummy!' I cried. 'I found it on the floor.'

'Well we must give it back to whoever dropped it,' she said, she was too honest.

'I don't know who dropped it,' I cried out in exasperation at giving her a small fortune. 'It could have been anyone, besides if you said that it was a prize like this, I'll bet that over a hundred people would say that they had bought and then dropped the ticket.' She saw the logic of this and accepted that fate had played us a winning card and I mentally hugged myself at having had my wish come true. This was the conclusive proof that I was a witch and could wish and get whatever I wanted in future.

It took two weeks but we finished up with a cheque for that amount and now, having had time to think, it was parcelled out into various channels, the bulk being kept for future living expenses, but she set up a small trust fund to help for my later education, which was ludicrous as time showed.

It was a frivolous wish that I made on my tenth birthday, but one that many girls of my age then would make. I wished that I would grow up to be an intelligent and beautiful woman and have excellent health. By not having quite reached puberty, it took some time to show that this wish had been granted though the intelligence began straight away. At eleven and now coming to the conclusion that I wasn't really a witch, I began to have serious thoughts about what I should wish for on my birthday.

My wishes for the next four years were of no account and for my sixteenth birthday, mother and I celebrated it alone. She took me out to dinner at a fancy restaurant where she made it quite clear to the restaurant that it was my birthday. Flushed, I blew out the candles of the cake brought out for me and mother touched my hand.

'Make a wish darling,' she said. I then made a wish, verbally, so that it would happen.

'I wish that we will always be happy and that I can find a man to love me as much as father must have done to marry you,' I said, holding her hand and saw the tears come to her eyes as I reminded her of who she had lost those fourteen years ago.

As the years began to pass, I began making wishes to help others and brought fame and fortune to those that I knew deserved it. Mother included, with her then meeting and marrying a charming bank manager where I went and fell in love with his son.

It was two years after mother had got married that I went and did the same to my new father's son and a year later, just after my birthday, I gave birth to our child. I had wished that he or she would have a wonderful life like I had had so far but didn't know that that had been my last granted wish. I tried for several years to follow in having my wish come true, but to no avail and just hoped that my child had inherited what I once had and would see that the wishes be put to good use to help others.

The End

Never Again

I will never again kick a football. I will tell you why soon for I must give you a short history lesson first.

England was once a part of Europe, but before man or beast lived on our planet, it was a maelstrom of power storms and heavy seas. The sea being forced from the north by the high winds, created the channel but with the sea from the south being pushed north would collide with the sea from the north and would batter the south eastern coast of England.

Any soil that was in that part was washed away creating, not cliffs, but more what would be described as giant steps. The lowest one went in roughly three hundred yards up to the second giant step which was about fifteen foot higher and that then went inland for just over a hundred feet before it stopped at the base of the third giant step. This one went inland for around two hundred feet before it met the fourth and final step that went a long, long way inland.

These four giant steps were almost straight and level and completely devoid of any soil. A large bay was created too that stretched just over three miles from East to West and rocks slowly built up at both ends to stick out into the sea for and mile and a half.

Nothing happened here until the Romans came and from a lake many miles to the north, built an aqueduct that was alongside the second step, to supply fresh water to their camps and town they built, further along the coast. This aqueduct is still used today but for pleasure craft only now.

Then came the Normans and from then on, slowly, houses began to be built on the First Step for the fishermen to take their boats out from the bay to catch fish. This small community thrived as a fishing village for nearly fourteen centuries until the bay became so filled with silt and sand that the fishermen could no longer get their boats either in or out, so they moved away. The houses then finished up as ruins and were not cleared away until the eighteenth century and a new village was built on the first step.

This village over the years grew larger and larger and they were about to start building more on the second step when the railway train came into being for transporting of goods and people, so this second step became the property of the railroad concerns and two tracks were laid.

So any more houses to be built began to fill the third step whilst on the fourth step, a family who had made a fortune during this period, bought the land on this top step and built a mansion that overlooked the bay. In time, the family passed on and the mansion was given to the National Trust to try and maintain it, turning it into almost what you would call a museum.

It was in the early fifties the government financed the filling up of the bay to turn it into an airfield which came into effect six years later. The village was now really a town and they used the old name for it to be called Steptown. With the airport being built, two hotels came into being and these were built at the eastern end of the first step where all the shops were with houses being built where there was room. This became the High Street and had a slight downward gradient which was beneficial when it rained. The town also now has a bus service which serviced the High Street and the Third Step, this now being its official name for the postal service.

Trains ran quite frequently now as well as goods trains, the main station being at the eastern end where the two hotels were built. The town also boasted a fire station, a police station and a taxi service and another building next to the hotels which became the town hall.

My own house was in Third Step and because of where I lived, I managed to secure the position of being what is known as the curator of the museum up on the Fourth Step. It was from the museum that began the calamity that befell Steptown, and I was the cause of it.

I was in the museum and had led a small party of people around and I was down on the lower floor of the mansion when a young boy up on the next floor at the top of the grand staircase, dropped the football he had been carrying. I saw it come bouncing down and as it came down near me, I kicked it.

It was supposed to have gone back up to where the boy was standing, but it sliced off the side of my foot and went straight as a bullet and smashed its way out through a stained glass window. I was dismayed at smashing that expensive window and found out later what happened to that ball and the havoc it caused.

The ball bounced down from the Fourth Step and landed on a cat. This animal gave out a loud scream and shot off, only to be chased by a dog that wrenched itself out of his master's grip. With the dog chasing the cat, they turned into Third Step street where unfortunately there was a man up a ladder doing some painting of the house. The cat went under the ladder but the dog hit it. This made the man cry out as the ladder went sideways and he was lucky to be able to jump clear before it hit the pavement. But he went into a roll so as not to break a leg and rolled into the road.

A cyclist was almost upon him as the man rolled into the road and so swerved outwards to avoid hitting him, but only a few yards behind the cyclist was a taxi. The driver also then swerved out to miss the cyclist, but there was a bus coming from the opposite direction that saw the taxi swerve and so he too swerved away from the oncoming taxi and mounted the pavement on this other side of the road. Fortunately, there were no passengers aboard as it was a young man being trained as a driver so it only held him and the trainer.

But such was the violence of the swerve that the bus toppled onto its side and smashed through the fence and slid on its side down the embankment only to collide with an oncoming goods train. The train driver had no chance with the bus hitting the middle of the goods wagons, driving them off the rails. Then came the real calamity, for all these wagons smashed into two of the stanchions that held up the canal that was alongside the railway. These collapsed, breaking the canal in two.

At this point of contact, it couldn't have been worse for it was almost the middle between two sluices and them being fourteen miles apart, had no control of the water that came gushing out from the ruined canal. I haven't yet worked out how much water there was in the canal, but with it being five foot deep and fifteen foot wide and fourteen miles in length, was one hell of a lot of water. This was flowing out at an alarming speed and went hurtling down the High Street, smashing into shops as well as the houses on either side of the road.

It continued pouring out and down only to then cascade out onto the airfield and begin to flood the runway. It was also unfortunate that a plane was just about to land and the pilot saw the cascading water too late and couldn't avoid the flow that was crossing the runway as the plane landed. The quantity and force of the water made the aircraft slide sideways and made the brakes useless and it slid along the path of water until it collided with one other plane that was stationary or avoid crashing as it spun, into the terminal building.

All this took place within five minutes of me kicking the ball, and would cost at least sixty million pounds to get everything back as it was. The only godsend was that the painter, two men in the bus and the train driver only suffered bruises as did some people in the High Street without anybody being killed.

Because of that, I will never again kick a football.

The End

Spelling and Words

I was nearly five years old and it would just after the summer holidays that I would be going to a junior school. At the moment, I was just in an infant school, though really it was a crèche for we had others there that were much younger than I was. There were another four that were the same age as me and we had been taught to read and write by Miss Slocombe, no, it wasn't the one from the T.V., but just one of the mothers that looked after us while our own mothers were at work.

'Okay children,' she began, speaking to just us five as we sat at the small desks apart from the younger children. 'You will soon be going off to a proper school and I would like to see how well you can write. So this morning, you have a pencil and paper in front of you and I would like you to write about how you help your mother. It doesn't have to be long, just enough to fill the page.'

One of the others lifted her hand, 'Does that mean daddy as well?' she asked.

'If you help him, yes. You can write about him too,' Miss Slocombe told her.

So as the others began writing, I wondered what I should put down. I didn't know then that I was dyslexic. I studied this blank piece of paper, wondering what I should write and decided that it should be when mummy asked me to do a little bit of shopping for her. The shop wasn't far away from where we lived though I did have to cross the main road.

With that settled, I began to write my little story hoping that I would do well with it. After just a few words I found that I was chewing the end of my pencil and noticed that the others were doing the same as we struggled to write something that made sense.

I knew what I wanted to write but had to struggle over the words that I was going to put down on the paper, but eventually struggled my way through my little essay and when I came to the end, my paper was collected up with the others by Miss Slocombe who then sat down and read then and made little marks at the bottom of each.

The papers were then passed back and we had to each in turn, stand up and read out what we had written. I couldn't understand why at the bottom of my page was a minus sign and the number eight written there, but thought it better to keep my mouth shut at the time and waited until the others had read out what they had written about helping their mother until it was my turn. I looked at it again to notice that twenty two words had been underlined and wondered if this was the number that gave me a minus. I shrugged my shoulders and began to read out what I had written.

It's better for you to understand if I write it down for you.

"I was helping mummy in the kitchen when she asked me if I would pop along to the shops and get a few things for her. It wasn't a lot for there was only the two of us, daddy having <u>dyed</u> a couple of years ago. She had <u>ritten</u> what she wanted me to get and gave me enough money to do <u>sew</u>. With the money in my pocket, I left our house and went <u>of</u>. I took care when I had to cross the <u>rode</u>, making sure that it was <u>cleer</u> before walking <u>a cross</u> to the other side.

I went into the shop and asked for a <u>peace</u> of <u>meet</u> that mummy wanted. With that <u>rapped</u> up, the next thing was a small bag of <u>flower</u>. With those <u>fings</u> in my bag, nearly got my money out and remembered about the <u>ise creem.</u>

So I <u>payed</u> for this and left the shop to take care again in crossing the <u>rode</u>, and was soon back at home giving mummy the bag and the change. Mummy then cut up the <u>meet</u> and put it in a dish which I think is called a <u>cassrole.</u> With the <u>flower</u>, she made some <u>dumpings</u> and cooked these at the same <u>tyme.</u>

It was a lovely dinner and I helped with the <u>wishing</u> up before going to bed."

Miss Slocombe then gave out books to the other and placed a big one in front of me. 'I think you should read this and look up all the words that I have underlined and you'll then understand what you have written.'

After looking up the first couple, decided that I would have to ask mummy to get me a dictionery.

Author: the last word was deliberate

The End

Gremlin

Christmas in a bachelor pad is not really the best place to be in the festive season. I had a small Christmas tree on the table by the window, too small for fairy lights, but still had bits of tinsel draped over a few of the branches.

Beneath it were three wrapped gifts placed in descending order of size. A bulky one from mother, a second, from my sister and the third was a box from my girlfriend.

Shirley, that's my girlfriend's name, has a key to my flat, but I'm sure she would have woken me up if she'd entered during the night. But who is to say that there really isn't a Santa Claus, because the next morning, I found a fourth present under the tree. It was the smallest and therefore at the end of the line.

I made some coffee and went and sat down to open my presents, wishing myself a Merry Christmas as I sipped at my coffee. The first was a knitted jumper, the second, a Paisley scarf and Shirley's, the third one was revealed to be a set of cuff links with the Playboy motif of the bunny ears.

I chuckled at that and then turned my attention to the fourth and mysterious present. The card was unsigned and just read Merry Christmas. I opened it to find a set of car keys and on the fob was the insignia of the Jaguar car company.

Sure enough, parked outside was a bright red Jaguar two door sports car. I let out a whoop of joy and quickly got dressed, putting on my new sweater and scarf, went downstairs and stood looking at the car.

Red is not my favourite colour, but who cares when you get a present like this for Christmas. The keys fitted the lock and I opened the down and sat down in the driver's seat and closed the door. It was actually a four seater, though I wouldn't have liked to be a passenger in the back. It was really only big enough for one adult or two small children, and I noted that the odometer had only nine miles on the clock. Obviously from the assembly line onto the transporter, then to the garage and from there to be parked outside my flat. My first and only thought was that it must have come from Shirley, but I would find if this was true later in the day.

I inhaled the gorgeous smell of new leather before inserting the key in the ignition and turned it to be rewarded with the throaty growl of a racing engine. Into first gear and releasing the hand brake, I was off and running. What a delight it was to feel the throbbing power beneath the bonnet as I changed gears, speeding up at the lightest touch of the throttle as I raced it to beat the lights as they started to change. The ease at which she cornered and the instant reaction of the brakes when applied.

It was mid-morning when I set off for the eighty mile drive in my new car, and it wasn't long before I was on the motorway travelling westward as snow started to really fall. I passed out of the speed restrictions and opened her up, but held it at eighty miles an hour and could still feel it wanting to jump up into a higher speed. I was in the fast lane, overtaking other cars with ease when the engine suddenly cut out and there was an unearthly silence in the car.

I looked into the rear view mirror to see cars approaching me fast, so I used the indicator to pull into the next lane. But there was no familiar clicking noise or blinking light to show that it was working. I pulled over anyway, getting a furious horn blast from the car I cut up. I pushed down on the throttle but still didn't get a response. There wasn't any reaction from the brakes either, and so it became very dangerous as I then had to weave my way between two cars to get onto the hard shoulder. Fortunately for me and others, that there were no other cars broken down to hinder my passage as the rolling wheels kept moving, getting ever slower until we came to a standstill beside one of the emergency phones that lined the motorway. For that I was thankful, because I now didn't have to trudge a fair way in the increasing snowfall.

I used this box to phone the breakdown service that I belonged to and was told, when they had ascertained where I was, that I would be seen to within the hour. Though they instruct you to vacate a broken down vehicle on the hard shoulder of a motorway, I stayed inside the car. I would have been a snowman if I had have waited outside for the length of time it took before a van pulled up, its orange lights flashing. I had tried the ignition key several times while I waited, but to no avail.

I hopped out of the now cold car and quickly got into the warm cab of the mechanic's van as he filled out his form with all my details. Then we both got out into the snow and he asked me to unlatch the hood. He poked about under there for several minutes, checking the leads and such like until he told me to try and start it. I got back into the car and turned the key and she started immediately with that throaty purr. He dropped the hood and came to the window, which I wound down.

'Terrific! What did you do?' I asked.

'Nothing. All the leads and plugs were in place. Just one of those things. With a new car, you nearly always get some sort of gremlin inside.' I thanked him for his trouble, and off I went again, taking care of pulling out into the slow lane before picking up speed again.

I had just turned off the motorway when it happened again. Complete cut out with nothing working. Luckily I was doing less than half the speed as before, but I didn't have and run off space if there was trouble ahead. I couldn't pull into a bus stop area because I didn't have the brakes to stop the car and I wasn't prepared to ruin the car by running off the road. I crossed a road junction with my fingers crossed at barely ten miles an hour and then slowed as the road started to rise with a small gradient.

I put the car into gear to act as a brake, and with my coat buttoned up, trudged back to the crossroad where there was a phone box.

It would be an hour I was told before another man would be able to come to my rescue. So it was back to the cold car to wait for the second mechanic to look at my new car.

He eventually arrived and I told him the same as I had previously said to the first mechanic. Instead of lifting the hood, he sat in the car and turned the key and the thing started instantly. I was flabbergasted, and told him that I had been turning that key every five minutes to no avail.

'Must be a gremlin,' he smiled as he got out, leaving the engine running for me. I thanked him for his wasted journey to which he replied that he wished that they were all as easy to sort out.

I carried on to Shirley's house without any more problems, arriving nearly three hours later than I expected. I was loathe to turn off the ignition in case it wouldn't start again, but I couldn't leave it running all the time I would be there, so I switched it off. I could always stay the night at her parent's place if it wouldn't start again.

I spent a couple of lovely hours in the warmth of her family, having dinner and social conversation. Then I said it was time we were leaving because it was now eight o'clock and we still had to drive eighty miles back to my flat. Goodnights were said and we went out to the car. I opened the door for her and she got in and we buckled up our seat belts. The car started first time and it purred its way back to the motorway where I was able to open it up a bit on our way to London.

'Lovely car,' she said, stroking the leather of the dashboard.

'Yes,' I replied, smiling at the fact that she was still not telling me that she had given it to me for Christmas. I had not mentioned it at her house and neither had she, so I was going to wait.

We were silent for most of the way and the car kept up the steady purr and I turned off the motorway and began making our way through the residential streets towards my flat.

'Thank you for my Christmas present,' I said, unable to contain myself any longer.

'Did you like them?' she asked.

'Them? Oh, yes, they were lovely, but I meant this one.'

'What one?' she asked, a puzzled frown on her face as she looked at me.

'This one. The car.'

'I didn't buy it.'

At this point, the engine cut out and I lost all my lights. Shirley gave out a small scream and I had to concentrate very hard to keep the car in a straight line. I used the kerb and a couple of cars to slow us down, wincing every time I heard the crashing scraping sound as I brushed other vehicles, imagining how much the repairs were going to cost. As we finally coasted to a stop, I began to wonder just who had given me the car and how had they got into my flat to leave the keys. We eventually stopped and I banged the steering wheel in frustration as we were only a few streets away from home.

'Damn this bloody gremlin,' I shouted. At that, a large black thing emerged from under the dashboard and scuttled up Shirley's leg and over her shoulder to land on the back seat as she began screaming.

The scream she gave out was spine chilling and she kept on screaming until suddenly, her head whipped round, her hair slashing me across the face. The screaming was suddenly cut off in a crunching snapping sound as her head disappeared from her shoulders to reveal a grisly mass of flesh and blood. Her torso twitched and heaved in the restraining seat belt as gouts of blood spewed out to hit the interior roof, splashing the windows, the windscreen and me. I watched in horror as this hot blood splattered all over me and following the echoes of her scream, I could hear a slurping and crunching sound from the back seat.

The screaming started again, louder and louder and I realised that it was me doing the screaming. My head was then gripped as if in a vice as it was suddenly twisted round and in that brief micro second, on the back seat I saw.........

* * *

Four days later, a police car pulled up by a red Jaguar car that had not moved, as the residents said, in all that time. They couldn't see through the red tinted windows and the car was locked, so the two policemen forced open the passenger door. The smell of the vomit that these two men expelled joined that of the stench from the interior of the car.

Forensics examined the inside of the car very closely, but could not give any explanation as to what happened inside that locked car. Nor could they explain the claw like footprints left in the dried blood on the back seat. Neither could they explain where the missing heads were.

Gremlins?

That's all folks!

~~The End~~

Here is a sample from another story you may enjoy:

AMY REDEK
HOT EROTICA

No **W**HITE **S**now

My name, though of no consequence, is Julie Winters and the younger sister of April, though her surname has now been Summers after marrying Jack, who is now my brother-in-law. How and why she married a man with that surname considering what hers had been, I never had the gall to ask her.

They had been married for almost two years. During the first year, my mother died; and after another year, my father followed her. I was then seventeen years old and since there was no will written by my father, the house and any monies in the bank etc., were then passed onto both my sister and myself.

Rather than living on my own, my sister suggested that I live in her house while we sell our parents' house. This way, we could have a bit of money each. Since I still have a year of college education and being virtually broke, I agreed to her suggestion, and so I moved in, though for that first year, I spent most of my time at my college and it wasn't until I got my diploma, did I really move in to live with my sister and brother-in-law.

I didn't know then of the desire that Jack had for me, but later found out after living with them for three months. April had gone up north to see how an aging aunt was coping, I was left alone with Jack, who told me to stop calling him brother and use his name.

That first night we were alone, he suggested that instead of me cooking dinner, we go out for that evening meal. He was the perfect gentleman then and after a lovely meal, we returned home and he suggested that we have a couple of drinks before bedtime. I'd already had half a bottle of wine and thought that a couple more drinks would be okay, so I said that it would be a nice way to round off the evening.

Now I can't say if he spiked my drinks or not, but a lot of what happened, I cannot really remember. I know I laughed a lot as we had our drinks and must have been given some kind of drug for when he pulled me into his arms as we sat on the sofa, I had no objection to him kissing me. I must have liked it, with him really being the first man to kiss me and didn't even have any qualms about having his hand fondling my breasts as we kissed.

Nor did I object when his hand went inside my blouse and had it push up my bra to release my breasts and have his hand massage them.

Nor did I stop him from taking off my blouse and bra for him to kiss and nibble on my nipples. I think I enjoyed it since I stroked his hair as he sucked on my nipples and didn't stop his hand from wandering down over my stomach and moved down under the waist of my skirt to have his fingers enter my pussy.

I appeared to have enjoyed his fingers playing with me for I gave out a little cry when he pulled his hand out and didn't see him pull down the zipper of his trousers because he was still kissing me. He then took hold of my hand and guided it into his trouser that was now open. He pushed my hand inside till I felt his erection and hand him curl my fingers round that hard muscle of flesh and gently moved my hand up and down on it.

There is a gap in what I remember for the next thing I know, we were lying on the rug and I was no longer wearing my skirt but completely naked as he was. He was down in between my legs and had his tongue moving about in my pussy, licking and sucking on me. His tongue was also exciting my clit. I gave out a cry when he stopped doing that to me as it was really exciting me. He then started kissing my stomach first before slowly moving up, kissing me all the way until he was kissing and sucking on my breasts.

If you enjoyed this sample then look for **No White Snow**.

Also by this Author:

The Painted Sword

Cruise Control

Wild Pleasures

Lending My Beloved

Lady of Cuckolds

Lady of Pleasure

Lady Magenta

Sexually Overdosed

Meeting My Fancy Dear

Prison Sex Slave

Chasing A Shadow

The Hostel

The Island

Thirst for Drugs and Pleasure

Forgotten Identity

Grey Memories

Chronos: Time Machine

The Hard Bomber

Honeymoon Abduction

The Yacht Sins

Three for One

The Sex Brigade

About the Author

George Eliot was a famous writer, though at the time, only male authors were recognised. It was in fact the pen name of Mary Ann Evans, a female.

When I started writing, I thought that if a woman could use a male name, why, with me being male, why couldn't I use the name of a female? Though to be different, I made my writer's name from an anagram of my real name.

I wasn't the brightest spark in my school days and it was only while being in the Merchant Navy did I self-educate myself. That being mostly literature, classical music and artists, like Tolstoy, Chopin and Rembrandt. After leaving the navy, I had several jobs, finishing up by being a working boss using my own maxim that 'Management is the art of delegation.'

It's when I became self-employed that I began to write, though sadly, not many of my books can be published because of certain laws that forbid certain aspects of life. This never fazed me for I was really writing just to please myself having a wide range of the human psych.

Having written ninety stories, my only aim now is to reach one hundred. I give thanks to the publishers for at least putting some of my efforts out for others to enjoy as much as I did in the writing of them.

You may also like the books by these authors:

Corrupting the CHOIR BOY

INTENSE EROTICA

JACK RYDER

It felt embarrassing somehow to still be forced to wear this stupid black and white choir robe. The pastor informed me that the women's committee had insisted I wear it even though I only got up to sing solo during the noon service. That sort of creeped me out that a bunch of old church ladies wanted me to look like some young altar boy to sing a couple of hymns solo.

Margaret was sitting in the front row as she has since her divorce six months ago. She has made it a point to sit as close to me as she can. She has told me that she likes a good view when I'm singing. At first, I thought that she was just flattering me. But as time progressed, she has added little flirtations every week. If I wasn't so much younger, I would swear that she has been hitting on me.

At thirty eight years old, Margaret is still a smokin' hot redhead. She sort of puts me in mind of that "Lady Heather" character in the CSI TV series. Today she is wearing a very tight navy blue skirt. Although it is not exactly a miniskirt, it fits her so tight that I can barely keep my eyes off her gloriously sexy round ass each time we have to stand up.

Although her white blouse is suitable for church wear, it fits so tight that I can easily see the outline of both her 34D breasts. I can almost make out the edges of her areolas. But every time she leans forward, her blazer falls open enough that I get a good gaze at her tits. I find it curious that she has unfastened a couple of more buttons at the top of her blouse just before I'm about to get up to sing.

Pastor Boer was just beginning his weekly church calendar announcements. (Yes…that is really his name. He pronounces it BARE, but you can guess what most of us call him). As he was making a lame joke out of the mistake on the schedule that had been printed as pot-lick rather than potluck, Margaret leaned over just far enough that I could see most of her golden brown jugs. She was not wearing a bra and I could see most of both breasts except for her nipples.

I could feel a wiggle between my legs as I glanced up to find that she could tell where I had been looking. She was smiling as she reached over and gently laid her hand on my thigh. "Your singing always inspires me so deeply," she whispered as her fingers slowly grazed up my inseam. "I enjoy the view as well," she giggled softly. My body vibrated as a finger brushed across my now fully erect prick. "Go…inspire me,"

She chuckled just as the pastor announced my name.

I was actually really glad that I had the stupid robe on as I walked to the front by the choir loft. The robe would at least conceal the boner throbbing in my pants. I sort of had to slouch forward a bit so the robe would hang forward enough to cover the bulge. "Stand tall, sweetie," Margaret giggled softly as I turned to face the congregation.

Once Larry the organist started playing the anthem I had chosen, my dick went soft as I concentrated on the music. I deftly reached forward and quietly shut off the microphone. With my deep and bellowing baritone voice, I would not need it. I was nearly through the first verse when I made the mistake of glancing over at Margaret. She had a huge goofy grin on her face and her legs were spread wide apart.

The pastor always sits in a folding chair behind the pedestal pulpit while I sing. This way he is not a distraction and it gives him time to go over his sermon notes. It also blocks his view of the congregation. I was the only one in the church that could see that she was not wearing panties. I was the only one that could see her bare bald pussy.

I was so distracted by the muff shot that Margaret was giving me, that I accidently skipped to the 3rd verse of the song completely leaving out the second verse and the refrain in between. My face was as red as a fire truck as I walked back to my seat with the entire congregation looking at me with curiosity. I was also sweating profusely even though it was fairly chilly in the church. "Were you thinking something naughty?" Margaret laughed softly as I sat down.

If you enjoyed this sample then look for **Corrupting the Choir Boy**.

Just Plain Bob

Sharing Penny

hot wife sharing erotica

It was my fault and I admit it. I accept the blame. I take responsibility for my actions. I own up to being the cause, the driving force behind it all. It was my idea, I pursued it, I encouraged it, and the blame is mine. None of that makes it any easier to wake up in the morning and find myself alone in bed.

***

It started with an overheard conversation in the lunchroom at work. Frank and Ernie were sitting at the table next to mine and they were talking about two of our co-workers, Bill and Steve. Ernie is a little hard of hearing so Frank was trying to speak loud enough for Ernie to hear him while at the same time trying not to talk so loud that everyone else could hear what he was saying. As a result I was hearing what they were talking about.

"She actually fucked him with Steve sitting there watching?"

"That's what Bill said."

"Do you believe him?"

"Why not? He isn't the first one it has happened to. George in Purchasing and Mike and Sam in Accounting have done her. Apparently Steve gets his jollies watching other men fuck her and then he goes down on her when they are done."

"He eats her cunt with another man's cum in her?"

"That's the story I get."

"Ooh, gross!"

"I don't know about that. Have you seen his wife? I've heard guys say they would eat a mile of her shit just to be able to kiss where it came from."

"No, I've never seen her, but it wouldn't matter how good looking she was I couldn't suck on her cunt with another guy's junk in her."

Well I knew Steve's wife and I could honestly say that as much as I love my wife I would have to seriously consider Marsha's cum filled pussy if it would lead to my being able to fuck her. For the rest of the day as I did my job I wondered how Steve went about selecting lovers for Marsha. Or did Marsha choose and send Steve out to fetch?

Whatever the selection process, it was obvious that I wasn't anywhere on the list. I had known them both for several years and they had socialized with me and my wife Penny. We have had dinner at their place and they have attended barbecues at our house and I'd never known or even had a hint that they had a kinky side. But this isn't about Steve, Marsha and me; it is about Penny and me.

***

I was still thinking about Steve watching Marsha fuck other men when I started home that night and about halfway home a stray thought entered my head. I wondered how a man could watch his wife, just sit there and pay rapt attention, as another man drove his cock into her and made her squeal and moan and I knew one thing for sure – I couldn't do it! At least that is what I told myself, but for the next couple of weeks it seemed to be all I could think of.

In my mind I pictured Marsha on a bed getting plowed by me while Steve sat next to the bed and smiled as Marsha screamed out in pleasure. I saw me standing off to the side watching Steve suck my cum out of his wife while my dick grew hard and then I fucked her again. I was not even aware of it when the change occurred, but one day I woke up to the fact that the picture in my mind was of Penny on the bed and me on the chair and that I had an aching hard on. From that point on I spent a lot of time wondering if I could actually watch someone else fuck my wife and if it would be a turn on. Not that I would ever know because there just wasn't anyway on God's Green Earth that Penny or I would ever do anything like that.

If you enjoyed this sample, then look for **<u>Sharing Penny</u>**.

Less Than Yesterday

Lilith Jones

HOT ROMANCE EROTICA

"We said we wouldn't start a baby until we'd gone for a year without needing my paycheck," she said. It hadn't been a year, had it?

"Well, I wasn't talking about starting anything tonight. It's been more than eleven months. And, if we aren't going to make the goal next month, where is the huge expenditure going to come from? . . . Not to end a sentence with a preposition or anything."

"Ted! That's not really a rule."

"Yes, dear," Ted said, sounding like he thought she was trying to change the subject. He was probably right, too, but he didn't pursue the subject. Ted was, she kept reminding herself, nice.

Thursday, a few weeks later, she started a new disk of pills. That night, with Ted working late, she realized what that meant. If she did what they had agreed, it would be her last disk of pills for a good, long while. She thought for a minute about keeping them from meeting the conditions by dipping into her savings to buy a new, costly wardrobe. The account was in her name, after all; she needn't consult Ted. Really, though, she could delay the pregnancy more sensibly than that. She could tell him that she wanted to wait longer before they had a baby.

Then, though, she would have to tell him why. Even if she trashed her savings account, he would ask why. She did not want to answer. You could tell a guy you didn't love him anymore; you couldn't tell him that you still loved him -- but you loved him less. You certainly couldn't tell him that you were afraid to have a baby with him because you were afraid that you'd love him even less in five or ten years.

And she did want babies. She had been an only child of a single mother, and she wanted four. Ted, who had been the third of four, had warned her that she was romanticizing the experience. "Sure, I want kids. We'll have one, and we can decide about the next after we have some experience with that one."

That sure didn't leave her much wiggle room now. She wanted kids; she wanted Ted's kids. They might inherit his brains, and he would be a patient father. She wanted his kids, and she wanted to raise them with him. She just wasn't sure she wanted to be with him for another eighteen years to do the job.

But, if not Ted, who? She still loved Ted. Thinking that she might someday love him so little that she might want to leave him was no reason to leave him now.

Of course, single women had children every day. So leaving Ted wasn't deciding not to ever have kids. That was stupid, though. She was afraid of having a baby now because she was afraid of raising it as a single mother. She certainly didn't want to leave Ted -- merely feared that she would want to sometime in the future.

By the time that Ted got home, she was eager to see him, so eager that she was already in a sexy nightie.

"Have dinner?" she asked.

"Yeah. I brought you some left-overs if you want them for lunch tomorrow." She carried lunch; his cafeteria was so heavily subsidized that buying lunch at work was cheaper for him than brown-bagging it. Dinner after seven was free. Nothing was too good for programmers who stayed late. "Is it too late?" For sex, he meant.

"I adore Theodore." And, really, she still did. She hadn't used that silly couplet for a while, but it still applied.

"Well, I adore Jessica, too. Give me a few minutes, and I'll prove it." While he was in the bathroom, she took off the nightie. Then she got into bed and pulled the sheet up to her neck.

Ted got into bed without baring an inch of her. Then he leaned over and kissed her before resting on one elbow and slowly drawing the sheet off her.

"It must be Christmas. Santa brought me what I've always wanted." He kissed her again. Then his mouth trailed down to her right breast. His chin scratched, but the scratches were exciting. When his tongue and lips on her nipple had aroused her, she spread her legs. He stroked her cleft until she tensed.

"Ted."

"Yes." He moved over her and between her knees, which she raised. Then he opened her, filled her. "Jess." His chest hair tickled her nipples as he moved above her and inside her. She licked salt from where his neck joined his shoulder. Her arousal gyred upward with each of his strokes. The tension broke, and she thrust herself at him and around him.

"Jess," he said as she clutched around him. "Sssi," as he drove her into the mattress. "Cah!" as he throbbed within her contractions. He collapsed on her, and they gasped into each other's ears.

Somewhat later, he pulled himself off and lay on his side inches away. When she backed into him, he wrapped himself around her.

"You are," he whispered, "the sexiest woman in the whole world." They fell asleep in the spoon, although they woke on their own sides these days. She put the nightgown on and covered it with a bathrobe before cooking breakfast. They kissed lightly before going out the door on their separate ways to their separate work.

It wasn't that Ted ignored her satisfaction, she mused on the commute. He took care to bring her to climax every time. It was just that he brought her to climax in almost the same way almost every time. Ted was a considerate lover -- just as he was considerate about doing his share of the housework and letting her choose her share of their TV shows and her share of their entertainment and socializing. Ted was nice. Was nice enough?

If you enjoyed this sample, then look for **Less Than Yesterday**.

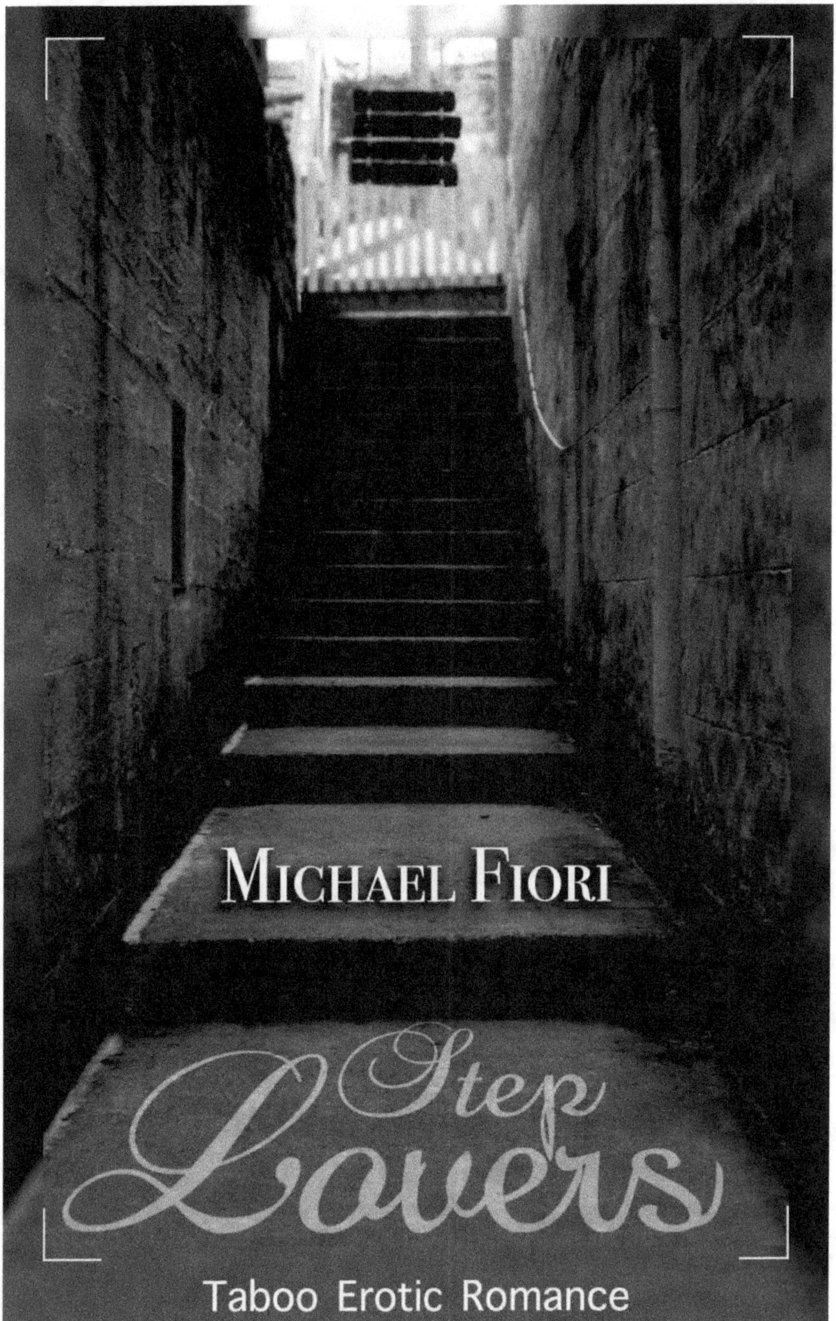
MICHAEL FIORI
Step Lovers
Taboo Erotic Romance

"Kids, we are out the door in five -- get a move on!"

The Alberts were hours away from their long-awaited and much needed vacation, and Mrs. Albert was getting nervous that she couldn't hear the rolling of her son or daughter's suitcases on the floor upstairs yet. 'It's probably Hannah making sure she has every one of her fifteen thousand bathing suits,' thought Mrs. Albert as she checked her watch and went through her carry-on in the kitchen.

A moment or two later and she could hear at least one of her children making its way down the stairs. It was Mark by the sound of it -- at around 6'2" and 200 lbs., the solid young man's steps were unmistakable. He didn't need to pack nearly as much, just a bathing suit and some warm weather clothes.

"Rio De Janeiro, here we come!" Mark exclaimed as he rounded the corner to join his mother in the kitchen. His mother thought to herself, what a handsome boy he had become, and he looked it in his sweater and jeans, though he'd obviously need to change into something warmer when they arrived.

Mark's aunt had been suckered into one of those time-share sales pitches and ended up with a few weeks in a beautiful Rio beachfront home that they couldn't make time to use. So when they offered a week to Mark's family, the four had quickly agreed to take the vacation together. Rio de Janeiro was supposed to be beautiful in February, as opposed to the cold winter winds of the Midwest.

When Mark's dad joined his wife and son in the kitchen, it was time to yell at Hannah once again, who replied:

"I'M COMING!" from Hannah upstairs, in an annoyed tone. Hannah stopped briefly and grabbed the sexy pair of black laced panties she thought she might get to show to one of the vacationing boys she hoped to find there. Her brother would inevitably be staying out late banging some dim-witted college girls as she knew he's used to doing; why couldn't she have a little fun?

High school boys could be so frustrating. Hannah had a few times thought about giving her cherry to a boy she'd really liked, but they'd all disappointed her somehow. Whether it was bragging to their friends, or treating her badly to look cool... every one of them just wasn't worth it. But it was no wonder that they kept pursuing her -- Hannah is a stunner. She had deep green eyes with large black limbal rings around them, which looked almost animalistic when she was scolding her brother. Hannah's thick brown hair looked good straightened, as she usually wore it; or tossed up in a ponytail as it was when she headed downstairs. Her family finally saw her rounding the corner to the kitchen, wearing tight black yoga pants and an equally tight Yankees T-shirt over her 32C breasts.

"You don't even like the Yankees!" exclaimed Mark as his sister came into view. His eyes widened when he saw how little her outfit left to the imagination.

"Oh, shut up, Mark!" She got so frustrated with him sometimes. He was always picking on her, and though she sometimes liked it (it was like flirting practice for boys at school) he often got on her nerves, like now.

Mark couldn't help himself most times, she is an easy target. Plus, it helped him to distance himself in his relationship with his sister. He often felt bad how turned on he got when Hannah's friends came to visit or sleep over. As a senior in college, he wasn't supposed to find their teen bodies and their scantily clad nighttime appearances so arousing. They were his sister's age, and she was a battle unto herself.

Every so often, Mark thought maybe he could excuse his interest in her, hiding it behind the fact that they weren't 'technically' related. Their parents had married when both he and Hannah were very young, making them step-siblings. But they'd still grown up together, fought and played together, gone to school together... No, for all intents and purposes, Hannah was as much his sister as any of the annoying princesses, aka sisters, his buddies complained to him about. Only most of them didn't have to put up with one like his.

Hannah almost never covered up at home. Mark had more than once walked in on her naked and brushing her hair in the hall bath, causing her to jump and her tits to jiggle as she shrieked and he mumbled an apology. He was guiltily familiar with the particular shade of pink of his little sister's nipple that showed when her loose-fitting tank top had drooped during a lazy day on the couch. And seeing the sexy brunette's petite frame tanning on their deck with her bikini untied... it was sometimes too much.

So Hannah and her brother typically kept each other at a distance, which helped to calm some of the storms that can arise between two stubborn teens living together at home. Hannah's mother talked to her once or twice about being more discreet around her brother, but it still seemed like every other morning that he was seeing her cute pussy lips peeking out at him as she bent over to put makeup in the mirror and he swung open the un-closed bathroom door.

Once or twice, Mark had slipped into the unwitting fantasy of closing that bathroom door behind him and teaching Hannah a lesson or two about being naked around him, but his senses got the better of him. More than twice he'd found visions of her swimming around in his head as he released a little pent-up steam in bed at night, but those he shook as soon as he realized their presence as well. And so, Mark did as he usually did when Hannah's tight ass had him wound up: he pushed the thought from his head, figuring that any 18-year-old with yoga pants hugging her cheeks the way Hannah's did would have his cock hardening the way it now was. His hardness made another appearance on the plane when Hannah's T-shirt rode up as she slept against the window, looking adorable. He gazed at her flat tummy before pulling the shirt down undetected. Brat or not, he didn't want the young guy in the next row checking out his little step-sister any more than he already was.

The family completed their travel about six hours after leaving the kitchen together, and they were tired. That long trip, cooped up in an airline seat or the back of the uncomfortable resort bus left all four family members longing for a nap before they arrived early afternoon. Hannah was the first to go for it after they'd ooohed and ahhhhed over the beauty of their temporary home. She pulled her T-shirt over her head as she sauntered down the hallway, revealing a comfortable cotton bra that Mark's eyes couldn't miss before she closed the door behind her and laid down on the soft bed.

Mark went to his own bedroom and dozed off to the image of his sister's backside burned into his eyelids: her wiry arms prying the skin-tight cotton tee off her body and the flexing of her beautiful back as she lifted her arms over her head... it simply wouldn't leave him until he was fast asleep. Even then it was Hannah's body that pervaded his dreams as he napped, his own little sister causing his cock to stand at attention for the better part of an hour or two before:

KNOCK KNOCK KNOCK

Mark rubbed his eyes and let out a yawning mumble, "Yeah. I'll be there in a minute!"

"Come on, sleepyhead," squealed Hannah.

Mark got out of bed and went to the door, his sister didn't seem like she was going to let up until he showed her he was out of bed. When he came to the door and cracked it open so light streamed onto his face, his little sister stood there on the threshold with her hip cocked, looking hot as ever. She was all prepped and ready to go, hair pulled back with a pair of sunglasses atop it, a yellow spaghetti-strap top holding up her beautiful rack, and jean shorts so short he could see the pockets peeking from below the tattered hem. She had obviously been working on her tan leading up to the vacation, and it made every inch of exposed skin a magnet for her brother's eyes.

'What the hell, man!' Mark thought as he rubbed sleep from his eyes, 'We've only been here an hour or two and you're already gawkin' at your own sis!' Mark had suspected Hannah was going to be showing off a bit when they got on vacation. She was starting to develop that curiousness that highschool girls have, when boys were checking her out everywhere she went. He didn't expect, however, to be one of those guys himself, but it was happening regardless. Thoughts wandering, he readied himself and by the time he emerged, his family was already walking out the door.

"Where are we headed anyway?" Mark called after his mom as he closed the front door behind him.

"Well," she replied, "since we always wait to go into town 'til the last day, and your father and I explored the grounds while you two were wasting time napping, we figured we'd go see what downtown has to offer."

Mark and Hannah beamed at her suggestion; they both figured they'd be more likely to find a cute boy or girl there rather than the resort. But Mark found one sooner than that; on the bus to the town's main street, a desirable-looking brunette caught Mark's eye and seemed to be sitting alone. Mark got up from his seat and approached her; he'd only just sat down next to Hannah and he figured she wouldn't mind. He cracked a joke and politely asked to join her and before long, the two of them were smiling and chatting like old friends. Hannah   did   mind, however. Mark's new seat had left her feeling awkwardly alone. Her parents in the row in front of them were flirting in that weird way they sometimes did, and it made Hannah want to gag. Instead, she turned her head and decided to get a better look at the girl Mark had found.

'That's just like him,' she thought with a twinge of anger. But it wasn't anger that struck her as she eyed up the new flavor of the week, it was jealousy, and it was causing her to start comparing the brunette's attributes to her own. 'My tits are definitely better than hers,' she thought begrudgingly, her hands made their way to her own breasts, feeling them to be sure. 'And she's not in shape at all,' she kept spinning. By the time they arrived downtown, she had analyzed every part of the girl without even realizing it and was sure she was prettier in every way. But then, like her brother, she had to scold herself for getting so worked up over her brother's new friend. Hannah thought maybe she just needed something to eat to cure her crankiness. But her wrath didn't stop there, or at the dirty look she gave the new girl as she stood giggling with her brother as they stepped off the bus. Mark's parents were prepared to give him a minute as they checked out the downtown, and then maybe let him go off on his own, but Hannah had no such plans.

"Daaaaddd, I want to go try on some clothes, can you ask Mark to come with me?"

"Honey, he's busy, I'm not going to interrupt him while he's talking to his new friend," her father replied. "Just come with your mother and me to this art gallery and then we'll go wherever you want."

"No way, I know how long I could end up looking at some silly painting with you two! I'll just go alone."

"Oh no you don't, Hannah," he retorted immediately, but she was already headed away from him and pretended not to hear. Her father then called after her: "You can't go anywhere around here alone!" But it was no use, she was obviously cranky and he knew that she wasn't going to listen to him when she was acting like that. So Mr. Albert, with a sorrowful look on his face, interrupted his son's conversation with the pretty girl and explained he'd need to run after his step-sister and be her bodyguard until she came around. Mark huffed and hawed, but in a few seconds, agreed to meet Emily, whose name he'd just learned later that night and took off after his sister.

"Hannah, wait up!" He said as he was about 30 feet behind her. She was about to turn the corner so he hustled and caught up to her.

"What's gotten into you Hannah, why didn't you answer me? I know you heard me." Mark asked as he grabbed her arm and she finally stopped her long strides.

"Well, excuse me; I didn't think it could be you calling me. You were so busy with that skanky looking girl you met on the bus; I didn't think you'd have found the time to come after me."

Hannah nearly winced as she said the words. She realized as they came out that they were a bit harsh, and she shouldn't be acting so jealous; it was only her brother after all. She looked up at him; her eyes had been fixed on her feet. Mark didn't see a scowl as he'd expected after that outburst, but a hesitant smile. He knew the look well; it was always his favorite way of avoiding a fight with her. So he put on a big smile and Hannah began to giggle as she always did when she realized she was being crabby.

"Let's get you something to eat," Mark said as he took her hand and they turned back in the direction Hannah had been heading. "But don't think I'm going to sit around while you try on ten thousand hats like we did in Mexico."

Hannah laughed as she remembered it, happy that her brother had joined her and left the bimbo who'd been stealing all his attention. She didn't like to admit it, but even though she and her brother had the occasional explosive fight, there was nothing like a good laugh with him; it cheered her up immediately

Before long, the two siblings were casually rambling the streets of the admittedly dingy town, though the delicious pastry Hannah was snacking on was a thing of wonder. As she felt the sugary sweetness touch her lips for the first time, she began to feel better; or maybe it was her brother's arm around her that did it. She could see why girls liked him. He was handsome and smart, and he was so good at making her feel the way she did now: happy. At a sleepover one night, one of her friends had suggested that Mark looked like Jake Gyllenhaal, and though she'd said she didn't see it, she had probably watched every movie he'd been in twice since. Once again, she felt grateful she'd pried him away from the other girl.

So they went on, walking and talking with Mark poking fun at Hannah for the pockets of her jean-shorts showing and Hannah clinging to her brother's arm like a child. At one point, with his arm wrapped around her, Mark felt the hem of her shirt rise up and his hand fell upon bare skin. He knew he should have moved it, but when Hannah didn't say anything he decided against it. Besides, it was an innocent touch, like the way his fingers moved all by themselves and pried at the waist of her shorts daringly. He must have just been feeling a bit turned on by the girl his sister had successfully twat-blocked him from.

They stopped in to a few interesting looking stores; Hannah tried on a hat at one of them to get a rise out of her brother and the shopkeeper threw them out when they bumped into a display as he grabbed it from her head. At one point, Hannah convinced her brother to come into a store with all kinds of clothing displayed outside. He sighed and ducked under a low-hanging wind-chime as he followed his sister in the store. She pranced about a bit, looking at this and that before going to the changing room to try something on. Mark had his back turned when Hannah came out.

"What do you think?" She said as Mark turned to face her. She stood posing in the same jean shorts, but an entirely different top. It looked to be knitted, probably by the woman standing at the entrance to the store, and it wasn't quite opaque. It didn't hardly cover half of her upper body, stopping halfway up her abdomen. He could see tiny gaps in the woven fabric throughout, with Hannah's chest peeking through at him. When he noticed the dark pink circles atop her perky breasts, he looked away.

"Hannah, I think I can see a little too much through that!" He exclaimed.

"Oh settle down you dog, I'll wear something underneath it, I just want your opinion."

"It looks real nice Hannah," Mark assured, looking at her kind-of sideways. His eyes stopped for a moment and Hannah looked down to see what he saw.

If you enjoyed this sample then look for **Step Lovers**.

Captivated & Rekindled Romance

Kerry James

Time Once More
for
Marilyn

Nineteen fifty seven was not a particularly notable year for the world, or for the inhabitants of the United Kingdom. Of course, there were quite a few people who would look back and say. "That was a good year, a very good year." But for many it was just another year. There were births, quite a few into poverty and starvation and the law of averages dictated that an equal number died possibly from that same poverty and starvation. In October the Soviets would launch the first orbiting satellite and the word 'Sputnik' became part of every language. This was a shock for every developed nation, particularly the Americans, as no one thought that the Russians had the technology to achieve that feat. We all got a year older, although some, like my mother celebrated her birthday and resolutely remained thirty five, ignoring the fact that she was born in nineteen eleven. The Spartan existence, we had known in these isles during WW2 and immediately after had relaxed and our family along with many others was enjoying a more comfortable life.

Our Prime Minister had told us we were never having it so good. At that time, in our innocence we tended to believe the politicians; later the scales would drop from our eyes. For the moment we went along with this fantasy. Most families had a television now and a refrigerator and if those were the yardstick by which to judge then we were indeed better off. There were jobs for all those who wanted to work and State Benefits for those who declined that activity. The Unions flexed their muscles to introduce socialist principles into Industry. They battled for those whom they called 'the workers' implying by inference that anyone who wasn't unionized was a shirker or a parasite or both. The 'workers' ironically spent more time not working; as their shop stewards frequently called them out on strike for the flimsiest of reasons. The Unions espoused democracy yet rarely let their members vote on strike action. The conflict between the workers and the management was a running battle that went on and on, ensuring years later the almost complete demise of British industry. If we were having it so good, it was a Fool's Paradise. However, for the moment we basked in the sunshine.

It was a surprise, therefore when my dad announced that the family was going away for a week's holiday. The surprise was that I was included. When I was young, we had family holidays. A week or two in the West Country, travelling there by train with accommodation provided by the euphemistically described 'Guest House'. A Guest House was one very small step above a boarding house. The furnishings were better, but the rules were the same, whatever the weather you had to leave during the day and not return before five o'clock. You were provided with bed, breakfast, and an evening meal, no early morning or afternoon tea. For me, the journey by train was the highlight. We travelled by 'The Cornish Riviera Express', the crack train of the Great Western, which, in nineteen forty-eight became the Western Region of British Railways. In those days it was still hauled by a steam engine, either a 'King' or 'Castle', gleaming in Brunswick Green with brass trim and copper burnished all glittering in the light. It was supposed to run non-stop to Truro in Cornwall, but it did stop at Plymouth. Not in the station, but just outside so the engine could be changed. The 'Kings' and 'Castles' were too heavy for the Royal Albert Bridge over the Tamar so they were changed for another, lighter locomotive. It was only later that I understood that during the holiday season there were at least three or four trains that left Paddington in the space of an hour and a half, all called 'The Cornish Riviera Express'. That did mar a little the pride in travelling on that special train. In the mid-fifties, my dad took a new job; moving the whole family from the London area to the Midlands. His position also allowed him a company car for private as well as business use. So the romance of the Cornish Riviera was now history.

If you enjoyed this sample then look for **Time Once More For Marilyn**.

www.ingramcontent.com/pod-product-compliance
Lightning Source LLC
Chambersburg PA
CBHW071338130626
46556CB00004B/1942